I love your sleepy wake-up **smile**,
it makes my heart go **ZING!**

I Love You, Baby

Claire Freedman and Judi Abbot

SIMON & SCHUSTER

London New York Sydney Toronto New Delhi

Three tiny words –

I love you,

seem too small for me to show,
how much I love you, Baby,
but I just want you to know . . .

I love our morning **cuddles**,
then our new day can begin!

I love your **funny** one-toothed smile,
your **kissable** sweet nose.

That **tickly-wickly** tummy,
and those perfect **wriggly** toes!

I love the **wonder** in your eyes,
at all the things you see.

The scent of pretty flowers,
as you hold one up to **me!**

I love you, love you, love you,

millions more than you can guess.
And nothing you could ever do,
would make me love you less.

When days are grey and chilly,
you're my **sunshine** little one.

We'll curl up with a story book,
for warm and cosy **fun!**

Peep-po and roly-poly–
we find fun in **ALL** our play.

If there are tiny tumbles,
my love **kisses** them away!

I love you when you **run** and **jump**,
and make a lot of noise.

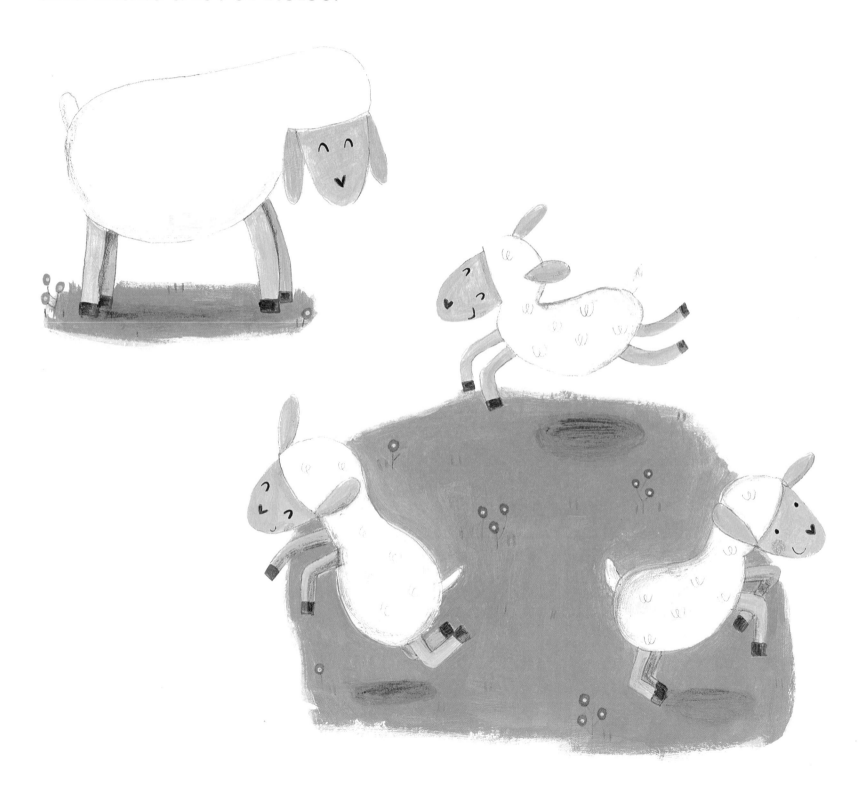

I love you when you're
quiet and **calm**,
or play games with your toys.

I love to keep you **safe** and **dry**,
in thunderstorms and rain.

I love our puddle **splashing**,
when the sun bursts out again!

My bright bundle of **happiness**,
you mean the world to me.

I love you higher than the **moon**,

and widest, deepest sea.

Each day is an **adventure**.
You'll make friends and have such fun.

But I'm always close beside you,
if you need me, little one.

So snuggle down and close your eyes,
the night is soft and still.

I love you, love you, love you,

and I always, always will!